Chuckie

by

NICKI WEISS

SCHOLASTIC INC.
New York Toronto London Auckland Sydney Tokyo

ISBN 0-590-32979-0

12 11 10 9 8 7 6 5 4 3 2 1   9   3 4 5 6 7/8

Printed in the U.S.A.   09

For Geri

Once there was a little girl named Lucy.

Lucy was a
good girl who
made her bed,

put her toys away,

ate all the carrots
on her plate,

and helped her
mama around the house.

She said "Please"

 and "Thank you"

and smiled when people said,
   "Oooh, aaah, isn't she cute?"

Then one day
Chuckie came.

"Oooh, aaah,
isn't he cute?"
said Mama.

"Oooh, aaah,
isn't he cute?"
said Papa.

"Oooh, aaah,
isn't he cute?"
said the nurse.

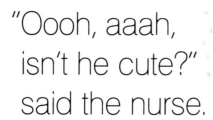

"Uch," said Lucy.

At first Lucy thought that if she wished hard enough, Chuckie would go away.

But then she would sneak a look under the baby blanket, and Chuckie would still be there.

Then she saw
the nurse packing
her bags.

Whoopee,   Lucy said to herself,
Chuckie's going back.

But the big nurse
left and Chuckie
stayed.

And stayed.

He grew a little fuzz on the top of his head and Lucy said, "Look, Papa, I think that Chuckie has some disease."

Chuckie began to eat food from a spoon and Lucy said, "Better watch it, Mama, or he'll eat all the food in the house."

Chuckie would wake up early in the morning and stare at his mobile

and Lucy would stand in the doorway and say, "Quiet, squirt, or you'll wake the whole house."

Poor Chuckie.

He was not exactly Lucy's idea of fun,
but he did not seem to notice.

He dribbled
his food

stupid

when
she walked
into the kitchen.

upid
stupid
stupid

He made noises

wowwooooo! *mooooomooo!* *blachhh!*

gaaaaaaa! *brzzzzz!*

when she
walked out.

If Lucy yelled
for her papa, he
would gurgle.

If she took a
cookie out of
his hand, he
would giggle.

"Oooh, aaah,
isn't he cute?"
said Papa.

"Oooh, aaah,
isn't he cute?"
said Mama.

He's just a dumb
lump of baby, Lucy thought.

Things were different since
Chuckie had come.

Lucy left her
bed unmade,

her toys all
over her room,

all the carrots  on her plate,

and she
refused to help Mama around the house.

Lucy tracked in mud
and said, "Chuckie
told me to do it."

She poured her milk down the sink
when she thought
no one was looking,

but then Papa
was standing there
and she said, "It was
Chuckie's idea."

She stayed up late
with her light on,
reading comics,

and when Mama
surprised her

she said,
"Chuckie said
he's scared
of the dark."

Chuckie grew and grew and the fuzz on his head turned to golden ringlets.

Lucy liked to pull those ringlets.

She thought that would make Chuckie cry.

But he only got hiccoughs from laughing.

At night Lucy would tiptoe
into Chuckie's room and
make scary faces.

She'd flip on the light

and say
BOOO!

And Chuckie would
giggle and giggle.

Chuckie began to sit up in his crib.

Lucy would come and push him over.

"Baby," she would say.

And Chuckie would sit right up again to play some more.

"I think Chuckie likes you a lot," Mama said.

"I think so, too," said Papa.

How do they know, Lucy thought,

Chuckie doesn't talk.

Nothing Lucy did seemed to bother Chuckie.
Nothing.

"Oooh, aaah,
isn't he cute?"
said Mama.

"Oooh, aaah,
isn't he cute?"
said Papa.

And then one night at the dinner table
Chuckie began to gurgle. He said,

"Googaa"   "Noonoo"   "Blachhh."
         and   and

Mama said,   Papa said, "Sssh!
"He's talking!"   Let's hear what
                              his first word
                              will be!"

"Oh, I'm sure it will be Mama," said Mama.

"But it certainly will be Papa," said Papa.

"Mama!" said Mama.

"Papa!" said Papa.

Lucy took a scoop of ice cream from Chuckie's dish.

Chuckie just giggled and said,

"Pkat"   "Plopf"   "Rszrszrsz"

and   and

and giggled some more.

"Papa,"
said Papa.

"Mama,"
said Mama.

"Oooh, aaah, isn't he cute?" they said.

Lucy took another
scoop from Chuckie's dish.

Just then Chuckie coughed.

Then he began  to gurgle.

 "Listen,"
said Mama.

"Sssh,"
said Papa.

 "Lucy," said Chuckie.

"What did he say?" asked Papa.

"What did
he say?"
asked Mama.

"Lucy,"
said Chuckie.

"Who? Me?" said Lucy.

"Lucy," said Chuckie.
He smiled. "Lucy."

From that night on, things were different.

Lucy made her bed.

She put her toys away,

ate her carrots,

and helped her mama around the house.

She also helped
Chuckie make
his bed.

She helped him
put his toys away.

toys

And best of all, she ate his carrots for him, sometimes

(when no one was looking).